keep her in your mouth

Poems by

Steph Castor

ISBN-13: 978-1-7345158-2-4

Cover design by Carolyn Brandt

Interior photos by Steph Castor

Printed in the U.S.A.

For more titles and inquiries, please visit:

www.thirtywestph.com

To having similar romantic sensibilities...

Table of Contents

Keep Her in Your Mouth

Bonus Land

Picture a corsage
made of 44 dandelions
picked to test the
lung capacity
of a 23-year-old;

the solace in a tickle war
with hair to match her name;

one hour
—scratch that—
half an episode of sleep
where you see flowers,
but bad guys pull weeds,
or maybe
it's the other way around;

every mile as a stilted dandelion,
while you're a weightless seed
—some "gossamer" wannabe
stuck to the cat's back;

a familiar tunnel vision,
like you're trying
to get your high in check;
a Ruby-throated loner
swarming the head;

a rhythmic reset
after a blood-thirsty
button mash,
where CONTINUE is
the only logical
decision,
and you're playing
for the story.

Passenger Seat

Aberdeen is her name
not to be taken lightly
you named her
for mountains
a harbor tryst
and pressed against me
leaned in
ribs deep in the railing

A reminder to
soak in it

The lighting
looks best
when you're dancing
It follows your hair
cascades down
your collarbone
Copper strands
pooling and spilling
over the empty space
your flux
is dying to fill

Reflecting

I fuck you
like I never want to hurt you.

"If God is real,
he's into this."

Triple Word Score

My arm
Cradles your whole head
Bicep flexed
I've been working out a little
Never enough
But maybe you can still tell
Need another pen
But can't let you move
Trying again
Shit
Orange
Just became
My favorite color
It's good news
Such good, good news
The way
You shove words
Deep inside me
Like a book
That needs to be fucked
If that makes sense
Book-cover blinds
Orange wash
Book-burn climax
Pillow talk
Book your flight
Nervous pause
Taste everything
Yes
Everything
Yes

So Close

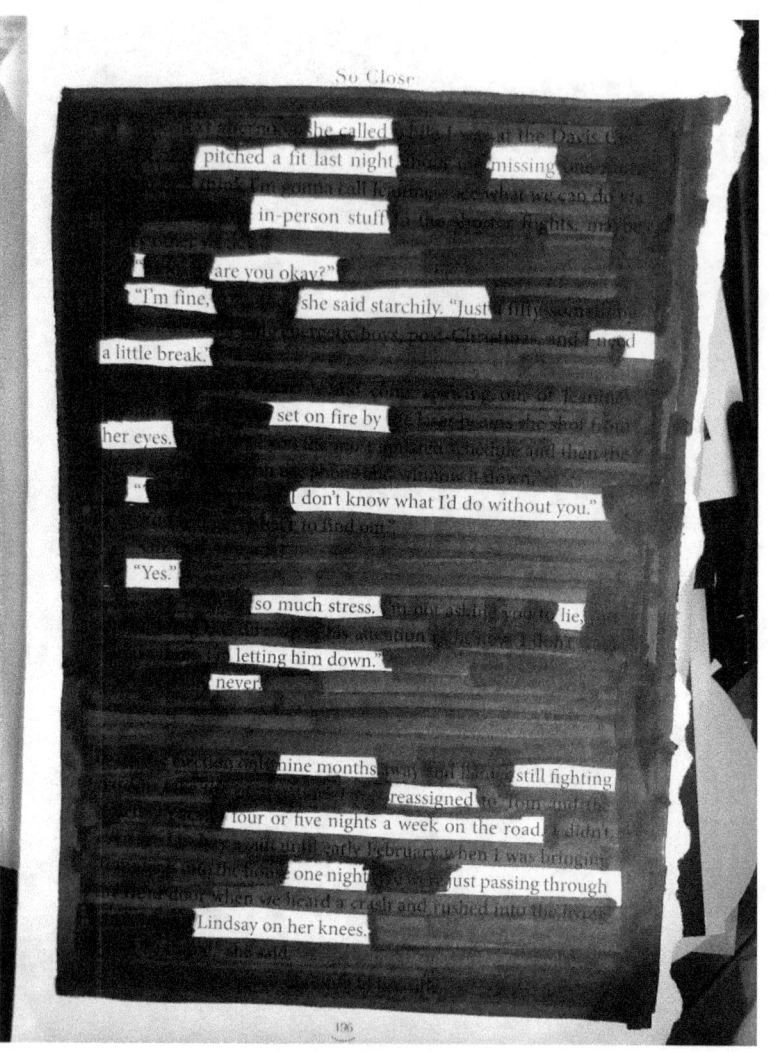

she called

pitched a fit last night missing

in-person stuff

are you okay?"

"I'm fine, she said starchily. "Just

a little break.

set on fire by

her eyes.

I don't know what I'd do without you."

"Yes."

so much stress. lie,

letting him down."

never.

nine months still fighting

reassigned

four or five nights a week on the road.

one night just passing through

Lindsay on her knees.

Cupid's Bow

You said
We should
Get a hammock
I assume
To complement
The perfect
Picnic basket
Your grandmother
Gave you
For them
Perfect picnic
We said
We'd only do it once
And that's okay with me
I'm more interested in
Sharing
The space
With you
Over and over
Making flashes behind
Our eyelids
Seeing how
We fare
Under new
Circumstances
Swinging in
The riverfront air
Curled in
Fall festival
Wind and decibels
Gritty and
Hair raised
On a nude beach
Spines curved
But contoured
Nonetheless
Deliberately shaped
Like Cupid's bow
Playful and precise
Like a mouth made for mine.

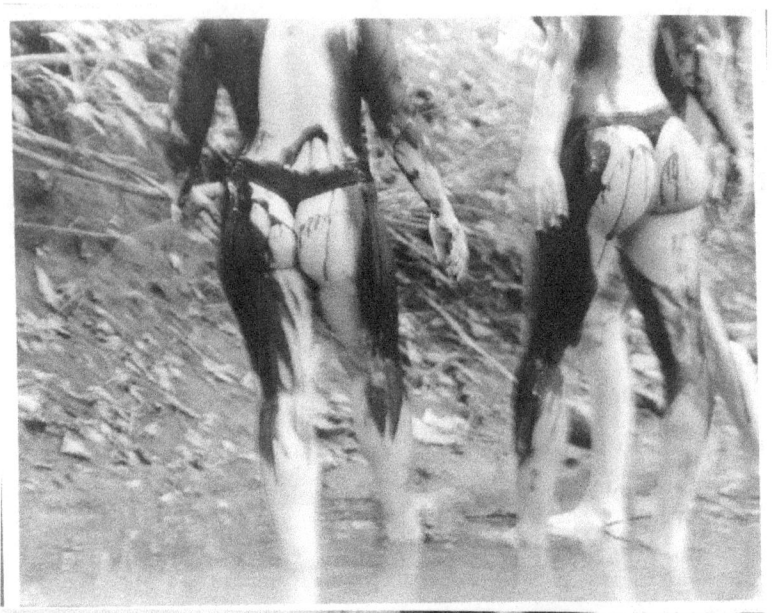

1126

If I had a key to every room

A bouquet would garnish each window

Peruvian lilies

Or something equally animated

When they are otherwise

Impossible to find

Some might call me crazy

For driving so much

But rest assured

I'm resting

And we are both

Smelling the flowers

How to Make Her Love You

The trick is
You can't
But you can
Preheat the oven to 400 degrees
Mention bacon mid-conversation
Have an eye for the
Perfect coffee tint
Write a book
Drive cross country alone
Knead fresh dough on her countertop
Clean the countertop
Shotgun a beer
For the first time
Look at family photos
Stack records
Make the bed
Drink Prosecco
Keep her in your mouth
Water the plants
Play card games
Plunge into a lake
Take mushrooms
Float on your back
Sketch pictures of birds
Know her favorite bird
Kiss her neck
Kiss her eyes
Kiss the corner of her mouth
Keep her in your mouth
Write naked in bed
Write naked on the couch
Just write
Fix your car
Get tattooed
Bring her coffee when
The color isn't right
Send her flowers
Smoke weed
Bring her weed
Give her time
Respect her space
Compliment the fern
Nurture the jade

Take out the trash
Wipe the sink
Light candles
Fold laundry
Pour a drink
Take off your bra
Introduce her to Mom
Keep sending flowers
Keep her in your mouth
Drink wine on rooftops
Go for riverfront walks
Pet all the dogs
Enjoy your job
Keep writing
Make more bacon

Moss

She is moss and masterpiece
dancing beside me
with hair to match her name

Earth-tinted glance
swallows rainbow-sugar syllables
she is moss and masterpiece

Wine-bottle galaxies
movie night memorabilia
with hair to match her name

A green-thumbed wanderer
houseplant synergy
she is moss and masterpiece

All business and candy
a dessert martini
with hair to match her name

Her core, a rose garden
jewel tones and Spring
she is moss and masterpiece
with hair to match her name

Slim Jim

I think it's sexy when you eat meat
Like the way you think it's sexy when I make it
You love it most with a little heat
A slow smoke oak pit

Like the way you think it's sexy when I make it
I come undone
A slow smoke oak pit
Meat stick pun

I come undone
And you pull me apart
Meat stick pun
Your mouth makes art

You pull me apart
Taste salt, then I bite into yours
Your mouth makes art
Fuck-worthy carnivore

Taste salt, then I bite into yours
You love it most with a little heat
Fuck-worthy carnivore
I think it's sexy when you eat meat

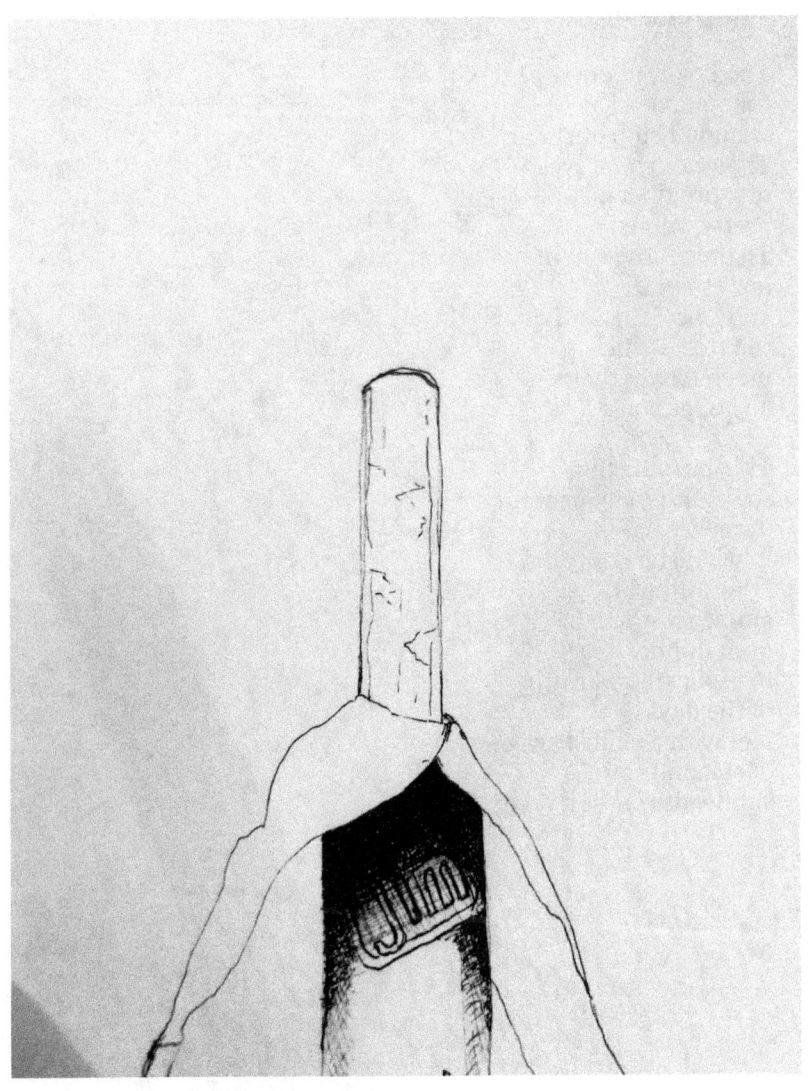

Mother's Day

The Polaroid proves
that our cheeks
wouldn't stop hurting.
That mom approves
of more than just
pretty women.
That with the sun in
our eyes
and smoke in our hair,
the stories stick
much longer than
any of us could.

This introduction
soaks through our walls,
drenches us
in what she now calls
"Dogshithead, "
and we just laugh,
even mimic,
to replay the warmth
of the day,
met with a chilled swig
of salt and sour,
subtle kisses—soft seeds.

Resistance (Goes Bump in the Night)

She is platinum.
She is platinum.
She is a monster
who writes songs
about monsters.
She is a platinum monster with blue eyes
and pink lips
and whiter teeth
than mine.
She is a pretty, platinum, blue-eyed monster
who tried to kill me a few times,
but not before
swallowing first,
hoping I would catch her
in the perfect moment
when her body felt like
a spent air pump,
warm and hissing.
She is a bourbon bottle,
also warm and hissing,
usually monstrous.
Have enough, and anyone is pretty.
Funny how
you become the monster
when all you hear
through all that hissing
is "worthless."

Paramount

I found a place to love from far away
as if you were blowing my dandelion arm
across the table

I can't stop studying you

light on your feet
at the Hollyhock

We identify every plant
and admire the olive trees
like freelance botanists

Your eyes glimmer, "land" subtracted
I'm caught off guard
and want to fall into your palms
like a ripe clementine
a citrus spritzer

You wear Hollywood like Hepburn

and bring it home with you
hold onto it
like the scent of Bronson Gate
or the sentiment of an autograph

You glow

You glow for good

Wax Museum

I keep saying she's all copper.
I must be confused.
Some call her the best crayon
in the box.
I suppose I would.
I do.
I made that up.
I'm the only one
who calls her the best crayon
in the box,
because I have the capacity
for wall-doodle
works of art
on an unsupervised
Saturday morning.
The TV bumps something
like Miley Cyrus:
some Disney anachronism
I am certain she would approve of,
even in diapers.
Even giving in to gravity
and plopping down on her ass,
shifting a bit,
taking a handful of wax;
curled wrappers—
all nubs and confetti at this point,
but somehow managing
to find herself
smearing them all over the baseboards
as if trying to spell a name
she has not yet understood,
eventually learning to appreciate it
and wear it,
complementing every color in
her wardrobe.
Here I am,
comparing her
to a child;
a fucking crayon—
once a metal.
I could never forget the taste, anyway.

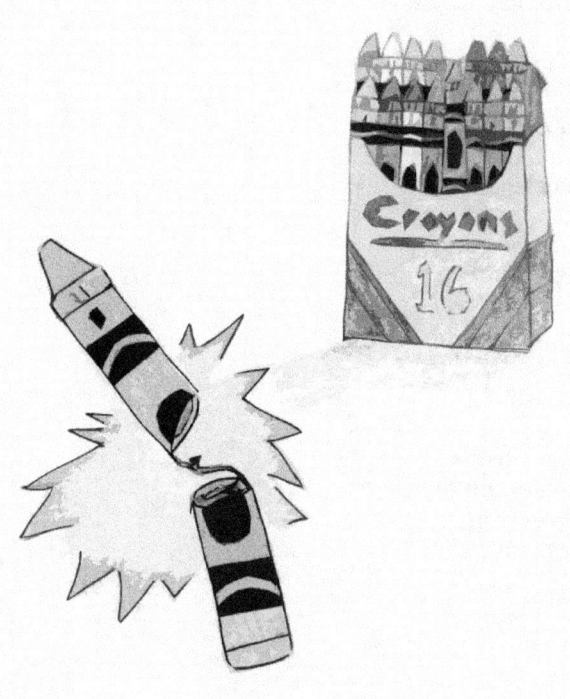

Old Tomato

When I was nine years old
I learned how threats are made
and how closets smell
if you mix a bartender's shoes
with dried cake batter.

The consequences
can be juicy—
Ripe
if you want to think about it
like a trait
that comes with age.

I learned how brittle
plastic hangers can be
when a grown woman
tries to break her fall.

Magical Thinking

Magic
is a word to be
broken.
You pick up
the pieces
and reassemble them
to make your own
sense
of your own
situation.
That's all
it ever is.
A situation.
A perspective,
reluctantly shared,
rarely welcome—
all in the
sting of
disbelief
and the wars
it could start.

No, that isn't my card.
No, that isn't my card.
No, that isn't my card.
Until it is,
and you have to
begin sorting
some shit out
together.

The magician
starts unskilled—
unrehearsed.
And you
are just
unopen
to the idea
that sometimes,
in order for things
to be whimsical,
you just
have to
participate
and not worry
about
the damned
trapdoor.

Time Capsule

I'd like to dig yours up,
forty or so years from now,
tucked under decades of dandelions
trounced by lovestruck children

I imagine I'd find assorted candies;
a lipstick-tinted joint
passed around a family holiday;
Andrew Bird ticket stubs,
still mint and carefully creased;
an award for Kansas City's "best hotdog"
pinned to an accidental Polaroid
of you with your mouth stuffed full;

and probably a copy of *Bedroom Music*
with a five-dollar bill
tucked in the dedication page
so I could enjoy a beer on you.

Jilly Bean

I'm still healing.
I put my phone on silent
to practice being alone.
It couldn't last more than
a few seconds
on any old clock,
but I'm not one to count time
in solitude.

Nothing gets easier as we get older.
We just run out of places to put things.
Start looking at our phones like
they're safety,
and the face next to you
is but a bigger threat
to your personal space.

It's like I'm biting into a piece
of blue meat,
but my stomach plummets,
and I lose my breath
on the first drop—
like a predator
that keeps watch
and prefers your smile
against moonlight
and serviette.

I wish
I could better convey
this warmth,
but I'm left
with a simple and expected
delivery
of weed
and sweater itch
on a blustery
downtown evening,
because I'm feeling
more cordial
than usual.

Don't you also feel
more cordial
than usual
when you rest your head
on my shoulder and know
what I'm contemplating
but ask me anyway?

Boxing Day

I came so hard for you that I cried
and woke up to salt crystals on my cheek.
I would have let you scrape them off,
because you're into that.
I noticed a small spot of drool on my pillow,
but flipped it over before you made fun,
and it's okay either way.
We loitered in bed,
knowing the door was locked
and your naked curve
wasn't going anywhere
until mine was.
But we both had mercy.
It's a long drive to St. Charles.

I do all of my aging in the car.
I showed you where I learned to park.
We worshipped the Corbett Canyon sunset,
soaked in sulfur til we both pruned—
were forced to untie my knots
and float for a while,
sometimes inside each other,
while sycamore leaves
garnished the photos.

We made time for the raspberries.
They are the brightest and sweetest
in the valley.
This is news to me.
And we both love raspberries.

I sleep in your bed—
or just on the couch.
It's the closest I can get
when you're gone,
and an only child
is a lonely adult,
which I've recently come to terms with.

We all thought Grammie died that Christmas.
Turns out she was just too high
and fell asleep
at the dinner table,
softly and subtly breathing.

I might as well have handed her a gun,
and she took a hit
without knowing the size of the bullet.
Mom said to call 911
—which I did—
but I would be lying if I said
I didn't first think
of how I needed you.
That moment of pre-panic
nudged into an uncontrollable
heart race
speaks volumes
about anchors
and what keeps us
afloat.

505

You insisted that I make a key
So I chose leopard
To match the shirt
That everyone loves most
Some say it brings out my eyes
I flash my key and say
"Try something more original"

I turn the deadbolt
And am welcomed by the unlatched chain
Already threading your loose copper strands
Through my buttons
Yellow Nerds
Wilted fern leaves
And hair
Coat the bottoms of my socks
You call that dirty
I still call it Home

Float

She said
"Don't ever stop, "
following my waking relief
to find her
soaked in yellow lemonade sun,
knuckles stretching
for soft knuckles
and tender thighs,
tongue settling
into river water tongue
—never mattered whose—
but the whole time, each other's,
and pretzeling.
We were all my favorite words.
Toasted summer snacks,
twisting crisp
and salty.
Properly hydrated
and coming down,
just to hydrate some more
and marvel at
the ducks dipping
their feet in the pond—
following leaders
and tapping their heads
before the great chase
alongside a smoke pit.
I'll always smile
for the displaced ferns,
the macramé,
and the fairytale we made
of it all.

Midway

Some trains have no shame in moving slowly.
It's a lesson to which we could all drink coffee
and color code our morning commute.

We rode the orange line first.
Not by choice,
but without hesitation.
It moved faster than I remembered.
I didn't feel her hand for long before landing—
the intermittent tightening around all joints—
unsure if she saw all things sinister
or spectacular.
I suppose they both inhabit the skyline and
kiss saucy-slurred passengers
with stolen deep-dish dabbed on their pant creases.

Why do I still find that sort of romantic?

I felt like her getaway.
It goes back to the take-off.
I was one Tank 7 deep,
and she sipped Bloody.
She held my hand as if to comfort me
or lend her expertise.
And, oh, I allowed it.
Her touch went from safety
to two fingers dancing at the base
of my thumb
and a restroom proposition
we never saw through.

Sunsets look like saffron
through her hair,
and for that, I'm happy to
offer the window seat.
She didn't mind that my nose dripped,
and I didn't mind that she fell asleep.
It gave me more ways to paint her.

I got to show off my savvy.
She conquered our check-in
and followed up with Lebanese.
We were six peach sessions
sloshed sour at the Music Box
during some problematic film noir.
But we stuck it out
just to say we did.

I've compared her to museums.
I've called her an exhibit.
Her old soul soaks straight to my core.
And I keep her history lessons with me,
buried deep as air pockets,
so really my stomach just never
stops
dropping.
I quote her
to catch my breath.

We love
looking down
from skyscrapers.
But I never told her
how scared I was of falling.
It was more like
"...I'll race you to the bottom."

A Self Love

You're more coordinated than you think
Strong hands
Clenching
Strings
Of all types
Nickel-wound
Bunny-eared
Bloody
Pulled to a stop
Pulled to knots
Pulled too tight
Tuned to snap
When played too hard
You prefer to shit in solitude
That's fine
You prefer to sleep together
Also fine
You prefer red over white
Unless you've tasted
The salt in the air
Where the grapes grow
And that is sexy as hell
Keep her in your mouth
If you can
Don't stop loving her
If you can't
Or simply don't want to
That's a threaded part of you
You are romance embroidered
By other
Strong hands
Tender hands
Blistered hands
Tired hands
Troubled hands
Hard, hard-working hands
That once knew how to hold you
And some that still do
Hold onto those
Don't let go
If you can't
Or simply don't want to
Or just because they know

For once
How to touch you
You owe that to yourself

To the Corner Fern, Always Watching

I was at some middle-of-nowhere
gas station
searching
for some middle-of-nowhere
postcard
that I had no interest
in sending
when I remembered
that freckle of hers.

Fast-forward a few hours,
driving through Colorado:
she called
on her walk to work
while I watched the sunrise
over sorbet hills
and breathed cow shit
—something we could laugh about.
She called me amazing
in an earlier message
I wish I could have kept.

She holds onto things, too—
keepsakes for a decade.
I'm honored to still hang in plain view,
appropriately positioned amid
jumbled Scrabble pieces
and an ever-changing
exquisite corpse
only better guests have played on.

I gaze at your empty post:
your secondhand chair by the window
where you saw so many scenes,
lost so many leaves.
I wonder if you're still living.
I wonder if you know things.
I wonder if you're rooting
in my favor.
I wonder if you could deliver
the same message for me,
but differently:
"I'm yours. I'm yours.

Always yours
in some good, good way.
Let me be a keepsake
that can't collect dust.
That can't be unpinned.
I don't want to be
in a box made of tin
with the scent of old chocolate.
I want to live in your smile,
the corners of your mouth—
the luscious parts only are known
by those of us who dare to ask
and want to put them
on every page."

Her space is a holy place
if I've ever known anything worthy.
The air is spring-like,
even with the windows shut.
It's thick with her belly laugh—
her light feet rapping on the worn
hardwood floors
as she rollicks and twirls
to King Princess
and still can't decide what to name you.

She dances across my body.
My face.
I start to spin, too,
and realize
I'm alone in the room
but still with you and your empty window corner.
Always with her.
Even on mute.
Close-captioned.
Paused. Rewound.
Let me be a keepsake
of ink,
asymmetry—
a synopsis
for a movie
that doesn't end.

Spit in My Mouth Next Time

I'm holding a hand that's not yours.
The conversation in the room is striking:
Fantastic Beasts, and giving head,
whether or not so-and-so has a gag reflex...
I don't know.
My heart is racing.
My face is itchy.
The cat's face doesn't look right—
like pudding: soft in the chair,
then firming up,
eyes farther apart than they were before.
Thanks to IKEA porn,
we've come to the realization
that no one should ever sit on
showroom furniture.
I'm having to remind myself to relax—
that my tits are not falling out of my shirt.
I'm feeling very focused.
Still preoccupied.
I think I'd like to go home.

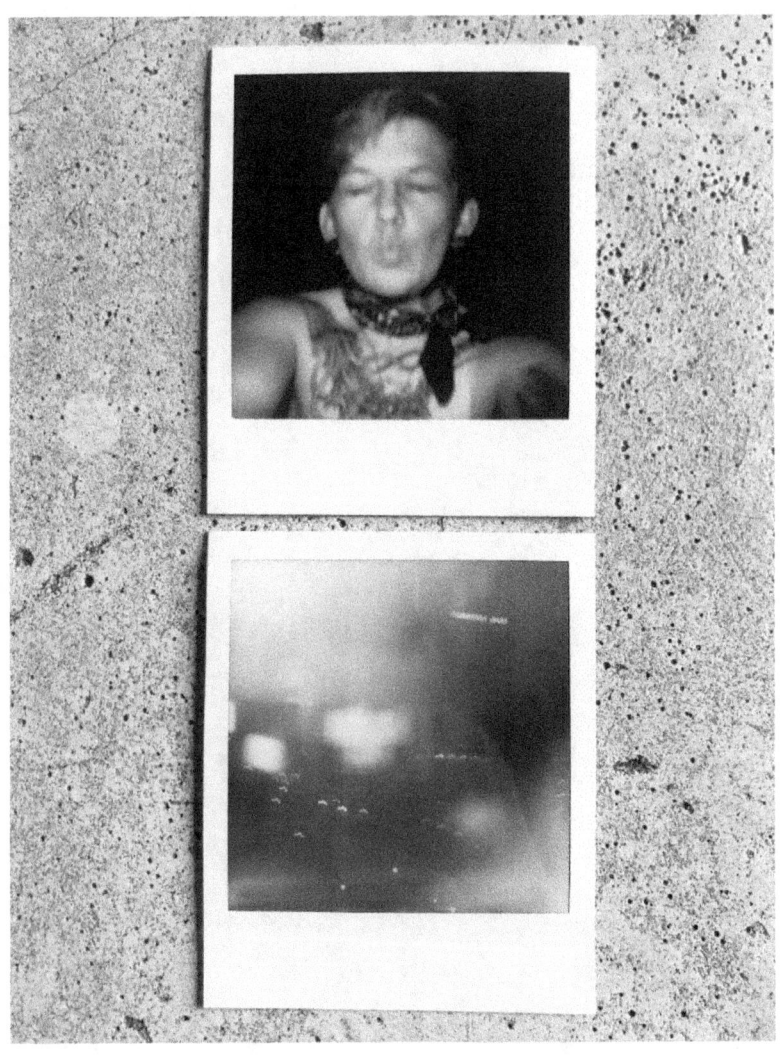

The Art of Garage Sale Conversation

Good morning
I like your look
My granddaughter's gay
Everything is half off today

Peanut Butter and Jelly After the Rain

I remember you

A soft Saturday sleep
Delicious dreams
Stretched calves
Across my waistline
Squeezing my bladder

September silly
A fanny pack of good habits
Brushing your teeth
At a Riot

Sonder

Do you look back at my window
when you're driving to the gas station?
Do you see me
when a bat flies past your succulents?
Are you able to make sense of it
and articulate it all better than I can?

Do you have long and deliberate
movie talks
on your walks with them?
I assume you walk with them.

I hope they make bacon.
I hope it's inferior to mine.
I hope it's perfect.
I hope they treat you right.
I have to assume they treat you right.
There's no room
for shitty bacon
when you're courting
a queen.

I have to assume that this stranger
feels everything.

Like I did.

Potty Humor

You asked me to flush your toilet
While you were out of town
That kind of talk is normal

I was pleased to do it

And to know that nothing gross
Was coming down the sides

I was even tempted
To scrub the mineral deposits
But figured you'd be anxious about it

Just know
That I would clean your toilet any day
Without even a hint
Of opposition

And that
Baby girl
Is true love

Whether you like it or not

Dear Letter S

I can't seem to shake you

I guess you found my love of patterns
And just went hard

It's more math than I'd like to work through

Born to two
Transfixed by three
With one phonetic exception
When you consider a soft C

And you can't forget my sister

Then there's me
The common denominator
With a love for consonants
And repetition

Fuck the numbers

The limit does not exist
Or something like that

My favorite letter
Makes exponents of me
Higher powers

Check my work

Massage Therapy

How many times
have you fallen in love
on a table?

Tonight
I let a real man
touch me,
and for the first time,
I have a hint
at how my love
must feel.

Fountain City Fixture

Kansas City is caked
with puke
and sororities—
tightly wrapped women
relying on red jerseys
and impulse.

I don't need to drink as much
to feel comfortable.

Doug knows my face.

Sergio knows my spirit.

I corner myself closest to fresh air
and ponder
just how gay
everyone passing
might be.

I allow myself to write badly
and clean up later,
increasing the odds
of catching your love charm
as it slopes past the neon.

Dough

one phone call
and I return
to good habits
gold thoughts
glitter heart
going soft
all
over
again
just
like
dough

I knew you
kneaded me

just look
at the way
I always
bounce back

Clean Sheet Day

What do you do in the blank moments,
the TV-14 stories,
and the wind chimes?
All you hear is a Hollywood echo
and reach for her hands,
wishing you could offer her
all of that:
the salary,
the screenplays,
the blessing,
the orgasms
upon orgasms—
like Portland was so five minutes ago.
Like Seattle was a warm-up.
And now you're wondering
if you should even lean in.
I'm not sorry our hands are the same size.
I'm not sorry for snapping photos of her stark.
I'm not sorry for a tighter grip
or for making zippers with our wet fingers.
I'll never be sorry for wet fingers.
I'm not sorry for kicking my shoes off
at the front door,
or for having to refold the sheets—
presumptuous as it seemed—
like I may have actually
lived there.

Eminence

I'm sitting at the bottom of the current—
ass dragging across smooth rocks,
moss,
lost sunglasses,
caps and stems—
wading with empty sandwich bags,
beer cans full of holes from summer Ozark shotguns.
I don't know how it got to be like this.
My body took a break, and now, like mud,
it sticks to shoes, palm creases, and pretty women—
peanut butter water,
jelly everything—
Psilocybin in my gums
chewed neat
like cow teeth
and swallowed
for much
prettier
pictures.

Curds

Why does
the smell of
melted butter
remind me of Australia?
I've never been
to Australia.

And I can't
stand it
when
other
scents
seem so tart
in comparison.

A year ago
we were
in room 1126.
Today
I received an email
suggesting
that
I
send
you
flowers.

Instead,
all I could
think about
was a pastry case
full of your
Sunday
appetite.

Trivia

My jellyfish chest
is pulp to your lips.
You, peachy monarch—
armed for battle with butterfly kisses.

We're different invertebrates but both just need to
go
go
go.

It took
new ways
of showing up for myself
to remember how one-liners work.

It took
remembering lyrics
to a Polka rendition of a '90s pop hit
to impress my friends.

It took
impressing you with random knowledge
to manifest my value at a quiet bar
and nail the bonus question.

Lamb Chop

I'm eating baby carrots to spite you.
Some say they pair well
with a rack or loin,
but you're all Chop and Charlie Horse—
cute in your
modest little spotlight
and tactfully
pissing in the back alley
through your overalls
when no one is watching.

Curbside To-Go

I'm at
John's Big Deck,
sipping Jameson
and water,
constantly
looking
over
my
shoulder
to catch your hair
whipping
in a warm
Kansas City
squall
long after
the storms
have passed.
This happens
just about
everywhere
in existence.
Perhaps
here
it is just
all too
probable.
Did I mention
that this
is the worst
name
for a bar,
like,
ever?

Cut Short

The bat signal

on the Commerce building

tells me you're home,

but I already know

from your Christmas lights

sprinkling

onto Baltimore Avenue

which I saw

as I drove home

with pineapple and concrete

on my breath.

This route

is purposeful.

It's how I get my dose.

It's how I soak

in the afterglow

of December;

of vineyards;

of a house built

for an actress,

named after a flower,

but never finished.

Please

reel back.

Take a walk with me.

Relish

that ice cream.

Because the credits

started rolling

far before

I could ever

be ready.

Skate Sunday

Some of us have moxie
while others enjoy edging.

Either way

we wear our tube socks
and coordinated outfits
like a mixed bag
of gummies.

We are an empire

of slow toe-stoppers
and high-waisted acid wash,

wrist flicks
and bruised legs,

razor burn
and road rash,

hard parts
and tight fades,

lipstick
and Taylor Swift,

broken arms
and blonde bangs,

slapshots
and sore asscheeks,

arcade goddesses
and lukewarm sex jokes
executed perfectly.

We are a gang
of cryptids
and public figures,

group circles
and talk therapy,

video games
and tarot readings,

pole dancing dilettantes
and former drag queens,

a shitload of Geminis
and some stippled Earth energy,

matching gold bracelets
and strawberry Truly,

tripping school teachers
and weekend dumpster divers,

We are the "Sister Wives of Sauer Castle"
and Midtown switches,

just bitches that wanna vibe—
Shut the fuck up.
You wouldn't get it.

We are rooftop rejects
turned Court Keepers,
and our thighs are looking great.

Scavenging

I'm sifting the rug
for shards
nose drippings
eraser shavings
chipped enunciation
crumbs of words
you forgot

Taxidermy

If I could bring you a bag of bones,
it might come with
a pack of menthols.

If I could bring you a dead bird,
it might be tied
to a bottle of red wine.

What happens when I want—you—
against the wall?

What happens when I want to be
in—your—mouth

or want you in mine

and am merely
days
too late?

Fill me

with your cotton
theory—
your textbook
instincts.

Be it
mouse or
fleshy body—

I could be
your next
big lesson

in anatomy.

In Response to the Unabashed Playlists by Vicky Martini...

I
f
o
r
g
i
v
e

y
o
u

f
o
r

l
i
s
t
e
n
i
n
g

t
o

N
i
c
k
e
l
b
a
c
k

Addily

I don't get along with ghosts.
I just love them
after four years
and nine months.
1,494 miles.
Three missed calls.
Do you remember
when you could count
the number of people you kissed?
What does Baby's Breath smell like
when it rots?
How many hits
will fix a fucked stomach?
I can't get off to the motion sickness anymore.

Scenarios

I heard seven gunshots

outside my window.

There was no response.

Nobody.

A little blood.

It could have been old.

I imagined how you both felt about it,

the conversations you might have

with your dad,

what you all would have for dinner,

and how strong of a nightcap you'd pour.

My brain is tired.

My brain is tired.

My brain is tired of wondering.

My brain is tiered.

My brain is tried.

My brain is dire.

My brain is direct.

My brain is director

and won't let up.

Shibari

I've been trying not to get tied up
by too many things at once
plans
people
projects
pussy

but it's all inevitable

when you're so focused
on becoming

and finally ready to submit
to the good stuff

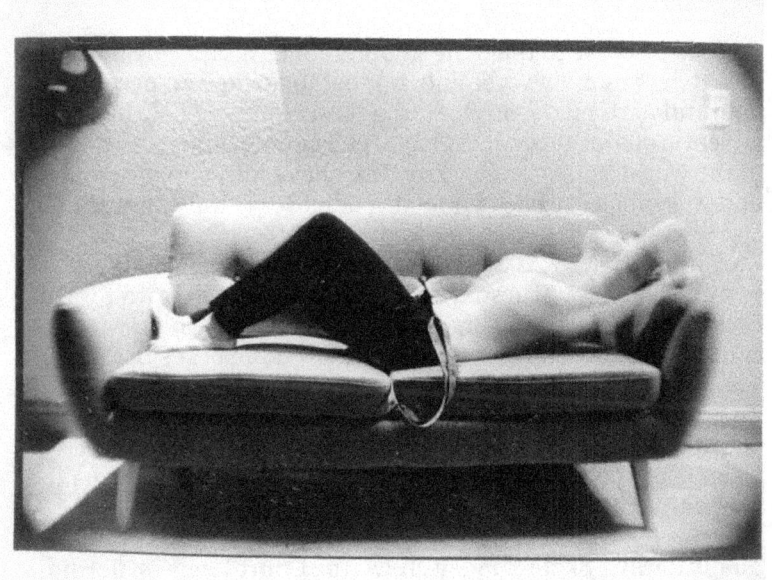

Acknowledgments

To thank everyone who played a role in the creation of *KHIYM* would take damn near another 80 pages. This year I learned how to experience people fully and what it takes to be truly perceptive. It turns out that deciding not whether but rather *how* to thank someone is perhaps one of the hardest things to do.

With that said, I would first like to thank Sienna Hohenstreet. You helped me rediscover and admit my worth. You inspired me to write this remarkable chapter of my life, believed in me throughout the entire process, taught me what love is supposed to feel like, and will always have a place to call home in my tender and syrupy little heart. I haven't stopped learning. Never will.

I would also like to thank my mother, Shelly Lara (the most heartfelt person I've ever known); her amazing and perpetually youthful partner, Jason Reeves; and my outrageously ballsy and adventurous grandmother, Patsy Lee Owens (known to the rest of the world as Grammie). You three have fully supported me and welcomed me back home through every kind of heartache.

To Sam Young, Rozz, Shantel Grace, and the Ramen Bowls family—you made Tuesdays something to look forward to. You carried fiery creative energy and lust for collaboration when I couldn't, and you all continue to draw out the best sides of me.

To Brie (Vaughn Ara)—you're pretty creepy, and I absolutely adore it. Thank you for always including me in your artistic visions and believing in my process. Your family has given me shelter and a refreshed outlook on daily existence.

To my darling Skate Sunday crew—the Court Keepers: Jordin, Vanessa, Syd, Markie, Paris, Kathleen, Carrie, Taylor, Anika, Adrian, KasiDee, and Kelley (last names purposefully excluded to uphold their true badassery)—you all genuinely gave me something to live for when all went to shit in the world. I am forever grateful for this chosen family and the support system we have created for each other. This kind of love is insurmountable.

Zoe Opal Green—you were probably the most magnificent and unexpected of all things. You reminded me of my capacity for romance at a time when everything seemed fleeting.

Josh Dale and the Thirty West team—thank you for seeing what many were too hesitant or afraid to digest. You gave this book a chance to breathe.

And, in no particular order, I'd like to express my infinite gratitude to the following beautiful and bold individuals who have taken a chance on me and contributed to this journey in one way or another: Nick Koenig, Jay Keim, Max Henley, Addily Dyer, Jessica Warner, Felecia Denton-Velasquez, Chelsea Harrington, Huascar Medina, Diana Rein, Kim Vodicka, Jeanette Powers, Jen Harris, Sondra Freeman, Rhonda Lyne, Midwest Music Foundation, and so many more.

We can all continue to survive this shitshow and maybe even enjoy it if we surrender control, embrace fear, and appreciate beauty from its subtlest and most unimaginative forms to its most frightening and humanizing manifestations. We are collectively poets, whether we like it or not—whether we want it or not. So we might as well share a good meal and get through this together. <3

About the Author

Steph Castor is a writer and poet of two collections—Keep *Her in Your Mouth* (Thirty West Publishing, 2020) and *Bedroom Music* (Stubborn Mule Press, 2019)—as well as an open-minded musician, novice photographer, half-way decent chef, passionate foodie, avid adventurer, and other (usually) intriguing characters. Castor spends most of her days in the local community darkroom, tearing up the Roanoke tennis courts with the hottest new queer Kansas City skate crew, or engaging in stimulating and satisfying brainstorm sessions with likeminded creative folks—often just for the rush. Past work can be found in favorite cultural and entertainment media outlets including *Curve Magazine, Guitar Girl Magazine, Guitar World*, Tattoo.com, and many more.